Field notes and sketches on Great North American Bears
by Alfred Clothears, Ph.D., M.N.A.S.

weight: 350-1100 lbs.
face: dished-in profile.
color: yellow-brown, dark brown to black, white on tips of fur.

eats: fish, grass, fruit, berries, elk, lizards, squirrels and snakes.

disposition: savage

range: Idaho, Utah, Wyoming, Colo., n.Mexico, N.E.Wash., Mont., Canada (Yukon, N.W.Terr., British Columbia and Alberta.)

Grizzly bear
ursus horribilis

weight: 200-500 lbs.
face: straight Roman profile, brown snout.

color: black, brown, cinnamon, blue. has blaze of white on chest.

eats: small animals, honey, berries, frogs, rodents, birds, pigs and garbage.

disposition: cranky, suspicious, disagreeable.

range: Northern Alaska to Mexico, most of U.S. and every province of Canada.

Black bear
ursus americanus

weight: 900-1400 lbs.
face: dished-in profile
color: yellowish to dark brown, white-tipped fur.
eats: salmon, insects, mice, berries, grass, moss, dead seals.
disposition: very dangerous, majestic and solitary.
range: Coast of Alaska, Yukon and British Columbia.

Big brown bear
ursus arctos

weight: 700-1600 lbs.
face: straight Roman profile, black nose.
color: white
eats: seal, fish, walrus, shrimp, foxes, birds, caribou.
disposition: bad.
range: Arctic regions and Alaska.

Polar bear
thalarctos maritimus

The Ordeal
of
Byron B. Blackbear

The Ordeal
of
Byron B. Blackbear

by

Nancy Winslow Parker

with drawings by the author

Dodd Mead & Company
New York

Grateful acknowledgment is made to:

Howard J. Lewis, Director, Office of Information, National Academy of Sciences, Washington, D.C.

The National Geographic Society for permission to publish scientific drawings based on those in an article in *National Geographic* magazine, Vol. 143, No. 1, January 1973.

FIRST EDITION

Library of Congress Cataloging in Publication Data

Parker, Nancy Winslow.
    The ordeal of Byron B. Blackbear.

    Bibliography: p.
    SUMMARY: A world-famous scientist's study of a
hibernating bear produces surprising results.
    [1. Bears—Fiction.   2. Scientists—Fiction]
    I. Title.
PZ7.P22740r   [E]   78-12140
ISBN 0-396-07642-4

Dedicated to a great lady of science,
Lois Bellinger de Alvarado, M.D., F.R.S.H.

Part 1

The Laboratory
of
Dr. Alfred Clothears

Dr. Alfred Clothears, world-famous scientist, had devoted his life to the study of bears (*Ursidae*).

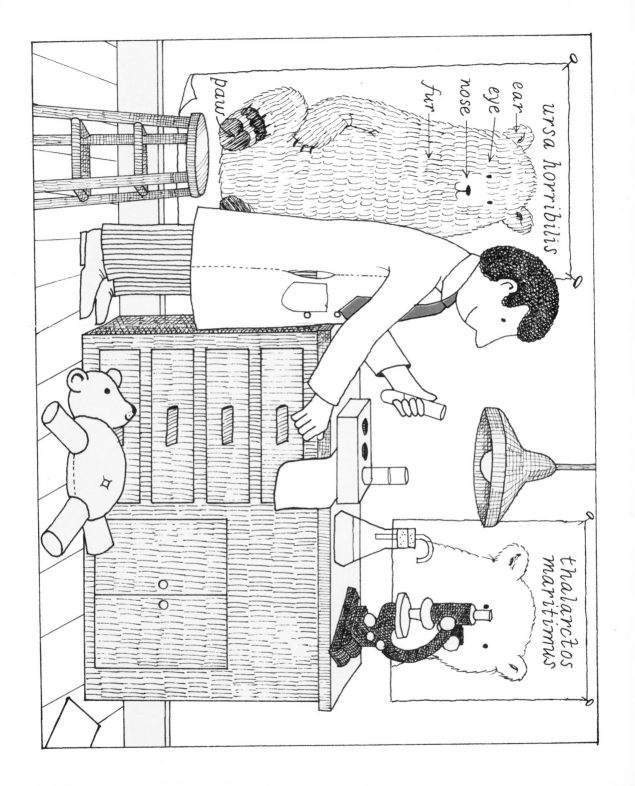

He knew everything about the huge, dangerous animals, except one thing—how they are able to sleep for five months every winter.

To know the answer would be one of the most important discoveries in science. Dr. Clothears decided he must find out the bear's secret.

He called in three of his colleagues and showed them his plan, Operation Sleeping Bear. They would capture a bear, then monitor the sleeping animal with the very latest electronic and scientific equipment.

They all agreed that the results of the experiment would be one of the most important discoveries in science.

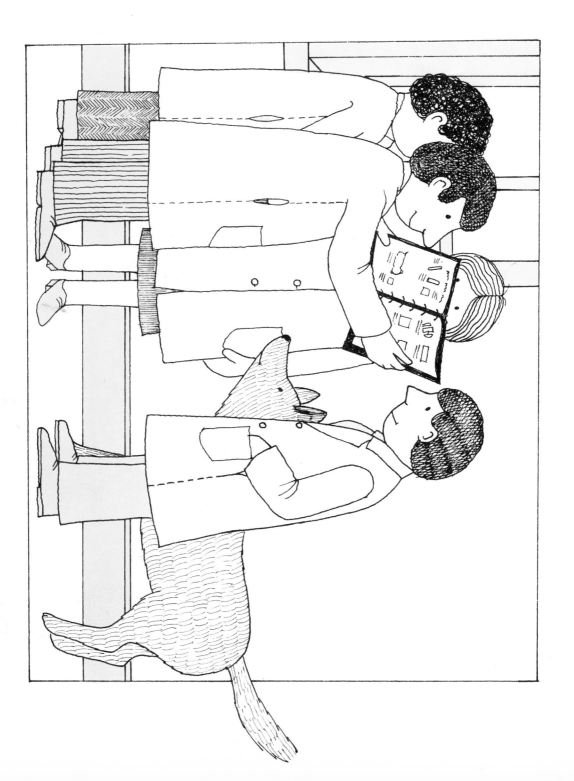

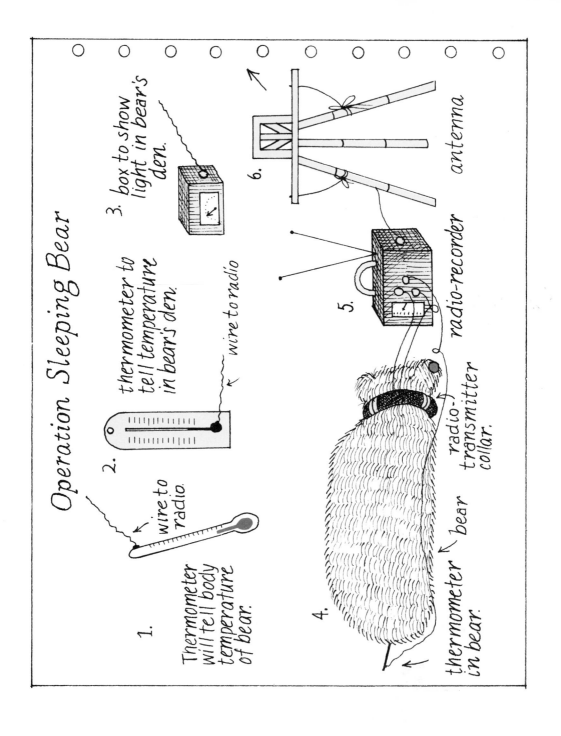

Operation Sleeping Bear

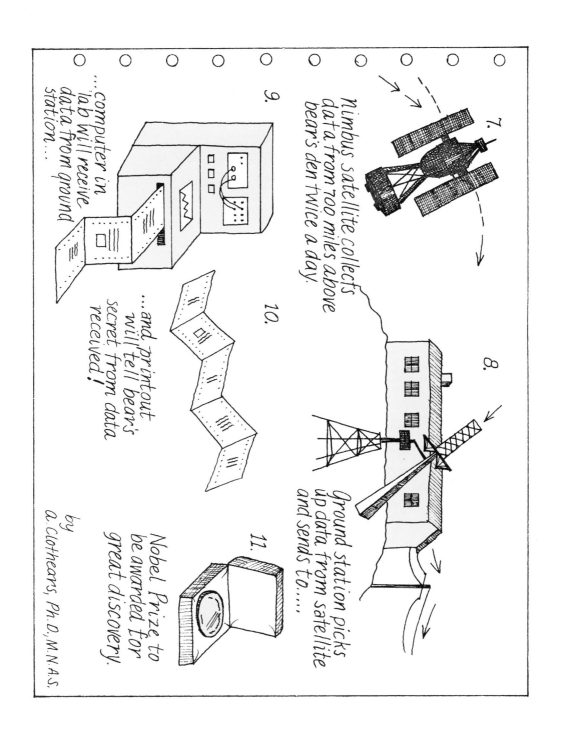

7.

Nimbus satellite collects data from 700 miles above bear's den twice a day.

8.

Ground station picks up data from satellite and sends to....

9.

...computer in lab will receive data from ground station....

10.

...and print out will tell bear's secret from data received!

11.

Nobel Prize to be awarded for great discovery.

by A. Clothears, Ph.D., M.N.A.S.

The next morning, the eager scientists set off for the north woods to find a sleeping bear.

Part 2
The Woods

Byron Blackbear was rudely awakened from his winter's sleep

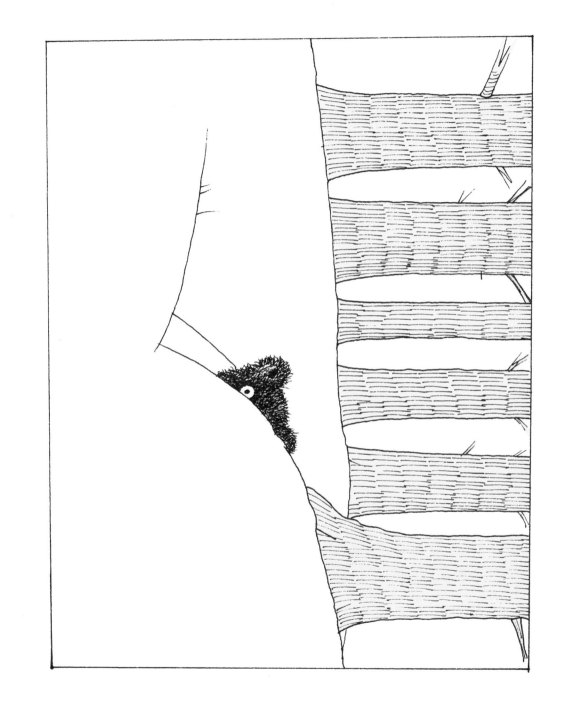

by a group of heavy-booted scientists,

who shot him with a tranquilizer gun.

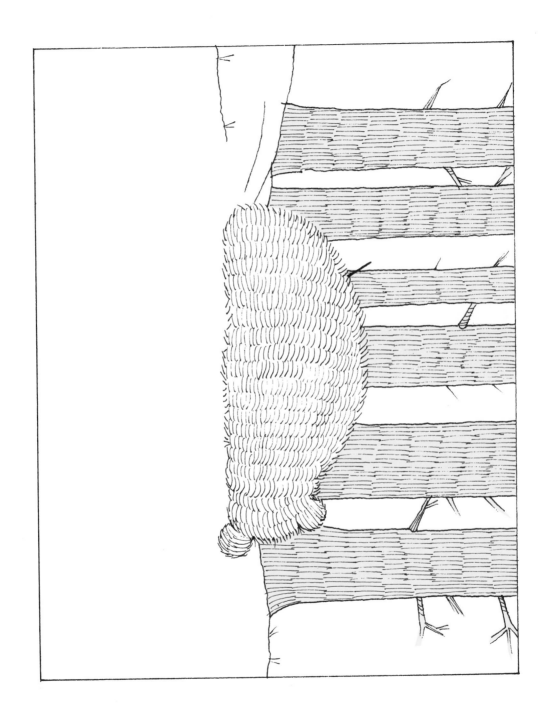

As he lay like a stone, they checked him over,

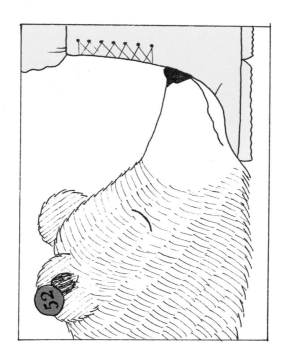

tagged his ear,

and attached their equipment to Byron's huge body.

Then they dragged him back to his den,

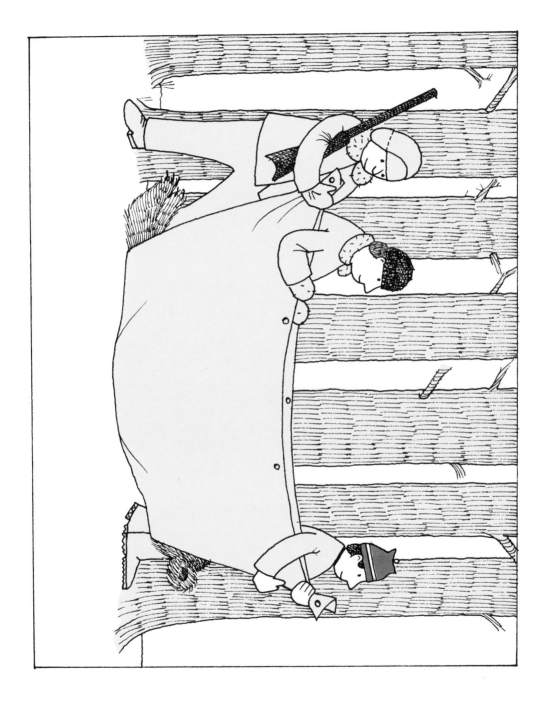

where they left him to sleep for the rest of the winter.

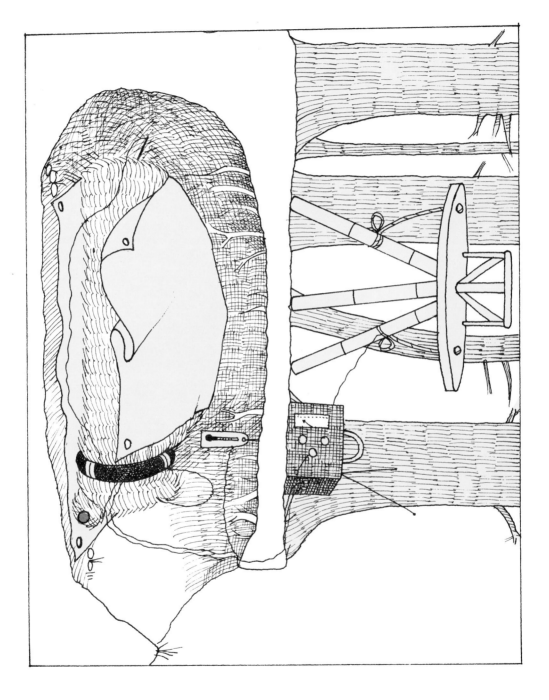

But Byron woke up shortly thereafter,

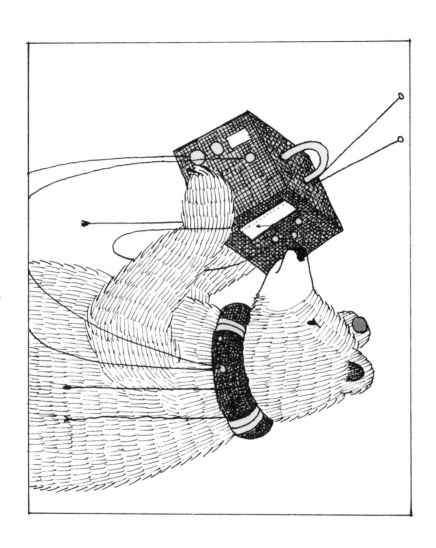

and angrily strode into the woods.

He gave the radio-recorder to a gray squirrel for a nut case,

the thermometer to a finch whose perch had broken off in

a severe ice storm,

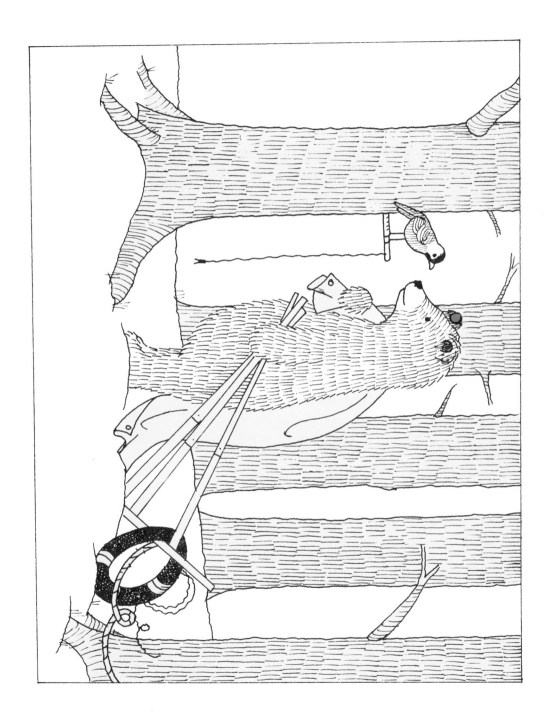

and the radio-transmitter collar went to his best friend, a moose.

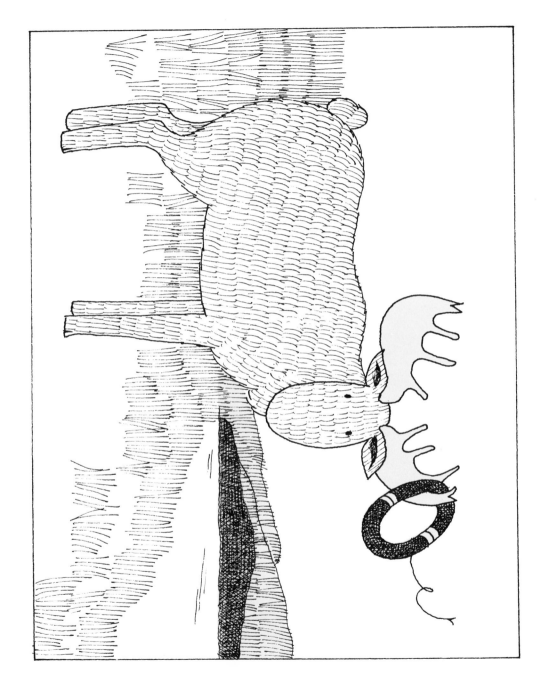

An enterprising beaver said he could use the antenna.

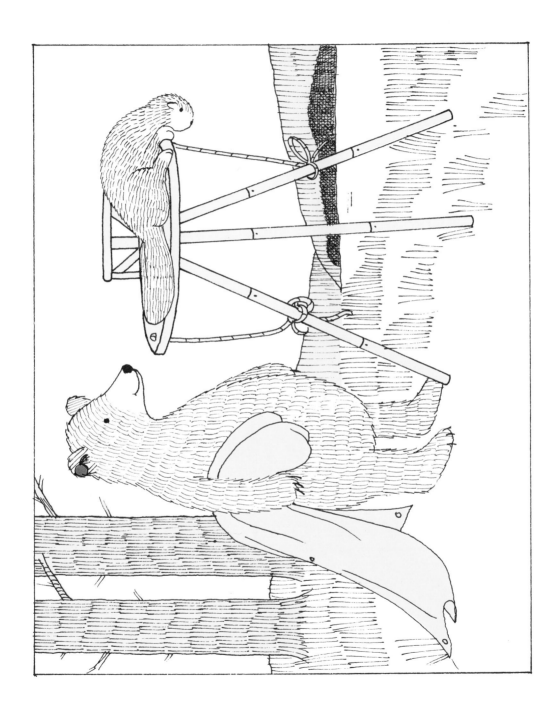

Then Byron wadded up the surplus U.S. Army tarpaulin into a ball, tied it up with some stout rope, and dropped it through a big hole in the ice.

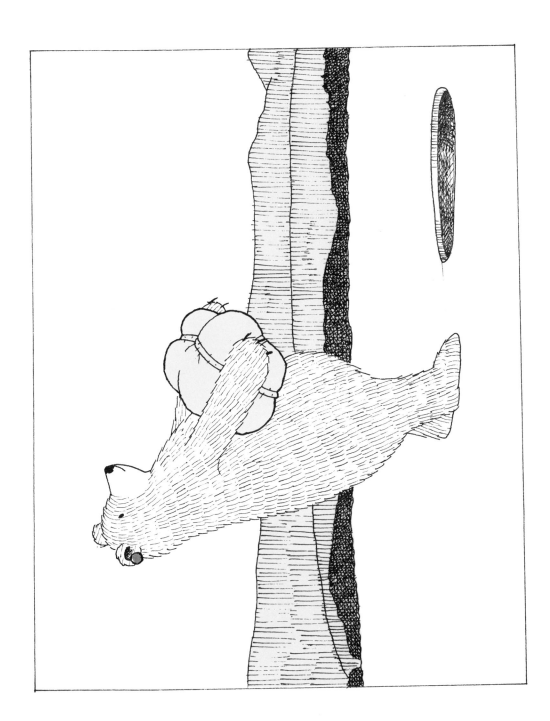

And then he went back to sleep for the rest of the winter.

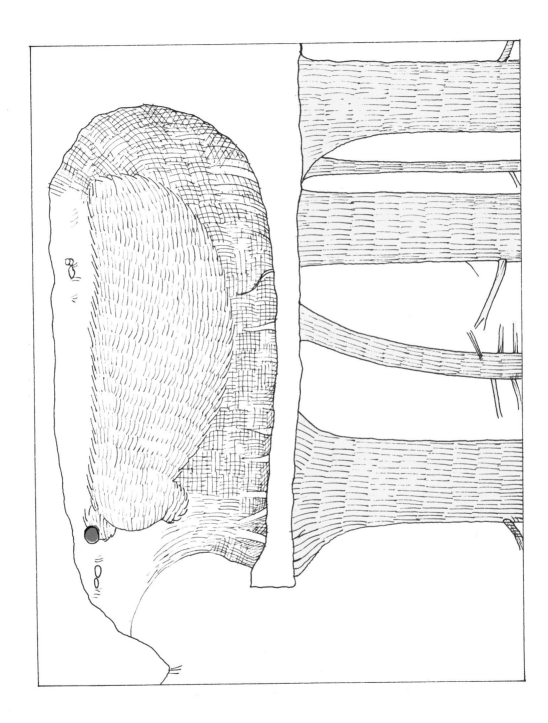

Part 3
The Laboratory
of
Dr. Alfred Clothears,
Several days later

Dr. Alfred Clothears, working late into the night on his notes,

turned on the computer, hoping to learn the secret of the sleeping bear.

The computer printout said:

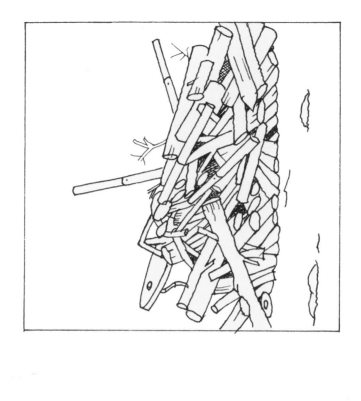

The antenna is part of a dam across the north fork of the Nooksack River.

The radio-recorder is in the hollow of an old fir tree.

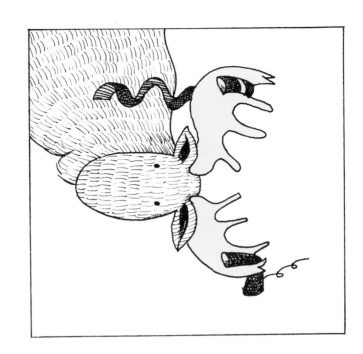

The radio collar was destroyed when a moose locked antlers with a rival.

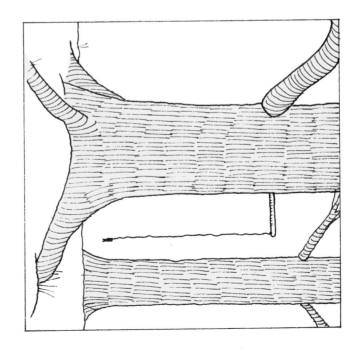

The thermometer is frozen into the bark of a red cedar tree and registers −20° C.

Dr. Clothears decided not to tell his colleagues.

The next morning, Dr. Clothears began studying the American dog tick (*Dermacentor variabilis*).

A Selected Bibliography

Beebe, B. F. and Johnson, James Ralph. *American Bears*. New York: David McKay Co., Inc., 1965.

Caras, Roger A. *North American Mammals*. Des Moines, Iowa: Meredith Press, 1967.

Craighead, Frank, Jr., and Craighead, John. "Studying Wildlife by Satellite," *National Geographic*, January, 1973.

Craighead, Frank and Craighead, John. "Trailing Grizzlies by Radio," *National Geographic*, August, 1966.

Egbert, Allen L. and Luque, Michael H. "Alaska's Big Brown Bears," *National Geographic*, September, 1975.

Wormer, Joe Van. *The World of the Black Bear*. Philadelphia: J. B. Lippincott Company, 1966.

Olympic black bear (Byron B. Blackbear)
ursus americanus altifrontalis

length: 5'
height at shoulder: 2-3'
note: straight back

range: Canada and Western Wash.,
Cen. and W. Oregon, N.W. Calif.

paw print:

Mexican grizzly bear
ursus arctos nelsoni

length: 6-8'
height at shoulder: 3-3½'
note: hump shoulder and long claws

range: Sierra del Nido in Northern
Mexico.

paw print

Kodiak bear
ursus middendorffi

length: 8-10'
height at shoulder: 4-4½'
note short claws

range: Kodiak Islands, Alaska

paw print

Polar bear
thalarctos maritimus

length: 7-8'
height at shoulder: 3-4'

range: Arctic regions and Alaska

paw print